CLASS
CLOWN

Other Scholastic Books by Johanna Hurwitz

Aldo Applesauce
DeDe Takes Charge!
The Hot and Cold Summer
Tough-Luck Karen
What Goes Up Must Come Down
The Adventures of Ali Baba Bernstein
Bunk Mates

CLASS CLOWN

JOHANNA HURWITZ

Illustrated by SHEILA HAMANAKA

A
LITTLE APPLE
PAPERBACK

SCHOLASTIC INC.
New York Toronto London Auckland Sydney

ISBN 0-590-41821-1

Text copyright © 1987 by Johanna Hurwitz.
Illustrations copyright © 1987 by Sheila Hamanaka.
All rights reserved.
This edition published by Scholastic Inc.,
730 Broadway, New York, NY 10003,
by arrangement with William Morrow & Co., Inc.
APPLE PAPERBACKS is a registered trademark of Scholastic Inc.

23 22 21 20 19 18   5/9

Printed in the U.S.A.   40

For David Reuther

CONTENTS

1

A NOTE FROM
MRS. HOCKADAY

The first Tuesday in October was very much like any other day in Mrs. Hockaday's third grade. Lucas Cott felt bored and restless. He always felt restless in class.

During social studies, he sat digging his initials into his desk with the tip of his ballpoint pen. The *L* was easy to make because it was just two straight lines. It was the *C* that gave him some trouble. He wanted it to curve evenly.

"Lucas is writing on his desk," a voice called out.

It was Cricket Kaufman, who sat in the seat across the aisle from Lucas. She was always spying on him.

"I am not," said Lucas, slipping his pen up the long sleeve of his shirt.

"Yes, you are," Cricket insisted. "I saw you do it."

Mrs. Hockaday came over to investigate. "Someone has written *LC* on this desk," she said, looking at Lucas.

"It could have been someone else. It didn't have to be me," Lucas pointed out.

"It is unlikely that someone else would bother to vandalize your desk with your initials," said Mrs. Hockaday.

"You didn't see me," Lucas protested.

"But I did," said Cricket proudly.

"Yeah? Well, it's just your word against mine," Lucas said, turning to face the girl who always seemed to get him in trouble. As he turned, the pen fell out of his sleeve and onto the floor.

"See," said Cricket, pointing to it. "There's the proof."

Everyone in the class knew that Cricket was

planning to become a lawyer when she grew up. She practiced all the time.

Mrs. Hockaday sent Lucas out of the room to get some wet paper towels and soap from the boys' room. "I want you to wash that desk as well as you can," she told him.

Lucas grinned as he rubbed on the desk. It was more fun doing that than social studies.

The day continued as usual with Lucas getting in trouble three or four more times. Just before dismissal, Lucas reached in his pocket and removed a drinking straw that he had placed there at lunchtime. He sat listening to Mrs. Hockaday reading, and at the same time, he pretended that he was smoking a cigarette. Once or twice he carefully tapped off the imaginary ash that was growing on his cigarette, as he had seen actors do in the movies.

Mrs. Hockaday looked up from the book. "Lucas Cott. What are you doing now?" She walked up the aisle and took the straw away from Lucas. "This is the last straw."

"No, it isn't," said Lucas, smiling. He removed a second plastic drinking straw from his pocket. "I have another," he announced. The class laughed and Lucas looked around the room, grinning happily. He liked to make everyone laugh. He had a reputation for being a real clown.

Mrs. Hockaday sat down at her desk and wrote a message on her personal stationery just as the dismissal bell rang.

As Lucas was walking out of the classroom, Mrs. Hockaday stopped him. "Please give this note to your mother," she said.

Lucas looked at the note. It was just a folded sheet of paper, not even put into an envelope. The temptation to read it was very strong. Lucas wondered what Mrs. Hockaday had to say to his mother. He waited until he was walking home before he opened the paper. Luckily, he had learned how to read cursive writing. The note said: "Please call the school to make an appointment to speak to me. I find that Lucas is very obstreperous in class."

The first sentence was easy for Lucas to read. But he did not know what the big word in the second sentence meant. *Obstreperous* had never been on any of the vocabulary lists that Mrs. Hockaday had assigned to the class.

Lucas looked around and saw Cricket waiting for the crossing guard to signal that the children could cross the street. Even though Lucas did not like Cricket, there was no denying that she was the smartest girl in third grade. Her papers were always neat and finished before anyone else's. And she was always waving her hand in the air to be called on. Cricket always had an answer and her answers were always right.

Lucas went over to Cricket and showed her the note. "Can you read this word?" he asked her.

"That's the letter that Mrs. Hockaday told you to take home for your mother," she said, recognizing the teacher's pink stationery.

"I'm taking it home right now," said Lucas. "But I want to know what she wrote."

"You shouldn't read letters that aren't addressed to you," said Cricket righteously. "I would never do a thing like that." Nevertheless, although the letter was not addressed to her either, she looked at the paper that Lucas held out to her.

"What's that big word?" Lucas asked.

Cricket sounded out the syllables. "It's a kind of doctor," she said knowingly. "It's the kind of doctor that a lady goes to when she is having a baby. I know all about it because my mother is going to have a baby next month. I'm going to be a big sister." She swelled with importance.

"I'm a big brother already," said Lucas. Cricket always thought she was so special. Wait until she discovered that it wasn't such a big deal to have a baby in the house. "I have two brothers and they are twins," he reminded Cricket. Then Lucas paused for a moment. An idea had just occurred to him. "Why would Mrs. Hockaday call me a doctor?"

"Maybe she thinks you are going to be a doctor when you grow up," said Cricket. "I could be a doctor if I wanted, but I'm going to be a lawyer instead. Then when I get older, I can be elected president of the United States."

"Well, I'm not going to vote for you," shouted Lucas, grabbing the letter away from Cricket. And then he ran across the street even though the crossing guard had not signaled that it was time.

"Young man! Young man!" the crossing guard shouted at him.

But Lucas kept on running and didn't turn back. He ran all the way home and proudly presented his mother with the letter from his teacher. It wasn't every day that he brought home such a fine note.

"I am going to be a doctor when I grow up," he announced.

"Really?" asked Mrs. Cott with surprise. "I thought you were going to be a wrestler."

"That was yesterday," Lucas explained. "Mrs. Hockaday says I am going to be a doctor that helps ladies make babies."

Mrs. Cott read the note that her son had handed her. "Oh, Lucas," she sighed. She read the note on the pink stationery a second time. Apparently she wasn't as smart as Cricket Kaufman, because after a moment she went off and returned with the dictionary.

Mrs. Cott turned the pages until her finger stopped at the word *obstreperous.*

"OB-STREP-ER-OUS. Resisting control in a noisy manner," she read aloud.

"Babies are noisy," Lucas agreed.

"Babies are noisy and so are you," said his mother. "Mrs. Hockaday is not at all happy about your behavior in class."

"I thought she said I was going to be a doctor," said Lucas. He could not believe that

Cricket was wrong. Cricket was never wrong, no matter how difficult the work was in class.

"You must be thinking of OB-STE-TRI-CIAN. That's a doctor. And you will never become an obstetrician or anything else until you settle down in class and do your work. Just look at your hands," said Mrs. Cott. "You must have been misbehaving to come home from school with hands like those."

Lucas looked at his hands. They were covered with pink, red, green, orange, and yellow stains. He grinned at his mother. "Claudia got some new marking pens and she brought them to school," he explained. "They are all different colors and they smell like foods. The red is cherry and the yellow is lemon. So I tested them and I tasted them, too."

"You tasted the marking pens?" his mother asked, making a face. "They could be poisonous."

"Naw," said Lucas. "Nothing happened."

"Lucas, you must not put things in your mouth unless they are truly meant to be eaten," scolded Mrs. Cott.

"Then they shouldn't make them smell so good," Lucas said. "The best one was orange. It smelled delicious. But it tasted blah, just like the others."

"Oh, Lucas," sighed his mother. "When are you going to learn to act your age? Did you do anything else naughty at school today?" she asked.

Lucas took a banana from the fruit bowl and began to peel it as he thought. "I didn't do anything," he said. Writing on his desk wasn't so bad, and it certainly wasn't noisy.

"You must have done something," said his mother. "Think hard."

"This morning I invented a great game," said Lucas, chewing a mouthful of banana. "I rolled my pencil along the desk until it landed in the little space on the end. Then I showed Julio how to do it and we had races. My pencil won more times than his."

"What was everyone else doing while you fellows were having pencil races?" asked Mrs. Cott.

"They were working in their arithmetic workbooks," said Lucas. "But Julio and I were having more fun. And besides, I had already finished all the problems Mrs. Hockaday assigned us. After a while, some of the other kids saw us and they began having pencil races, too. Pretty soon everyone was having them. Except Cricket," he remembered.

"Pencil races are obstreperous behavior," said his mother.

"But everyone was doing it," objected Lucas. "And I'm the only one who got a note sent home."

"Did you do anything else?" asked his mother.

"During USSR, Mrs. Hockaday made me sit outside the classroom on a chair in the hallway."

"USSR?"

"Universal Sustained Silent Reading. That's when everyone in the whole school reads at the same time."

"Oh, yes. I forgot," said Mrs. Cott. "Well, why did you have to sit outside? Weren't you reading like everyone else?"

"Sure I was reading," said Lucas. "But Mrs. Hockaday got angry because I was opening and closing the Velcro tabs on my sneakers. She said it was distracting everybody."

"It does sound a tiny bit obstreperous to me," said Mrs. Cott. "Did you do anything else today?"

"I called out the answers during English instead of raising my hand," Lucas admitted.

"That's bad," said his mother. "Suppose everyone called out the answers all the time. How could Mrs. Hockaday keep order in the classroom?"

"But if I don't call out the answers, then she always calls on Cricket. Cricket is so smart she raises her hand before Mrs. Hockaday even asks the questions. That way her hand is up in the air first. It's not fair."

"Promise me that tomorrow you won't have any pencil races or play with the Velcro tabs on your sneakers or call out answers," begged Mrs. Cott. "You're a smart kid, Lucas, and Mrs. Hockaday is so busy scolding you for misbehavior that she'll never have time to find out."

"Do you really think I'm smart?" asked Lucas.

"Of course I do," said his mother. "Don't you remember your father and me telling you how early you learned to speak. The twins are only able to say a few words, but when you were their age you were speaking in complete sentences. But sometimes it's better not to speak and just hold your tongue. Don't call out answers. Just raise your hand. You can have hand-raising races with Cricket instead of pencil races with Julio."

"Yeah," said Lucas. "That's a good idea."

A sharp scream came from the next room. "The twins are waking from their nap," sighed Mrs. Cott. "Enough bananas." She grabbed a banana from Lucas. "You had one already. You'll spoil your appetite for supper."

"Okay." Lucas sighed. It seemed whatever he opened his mouth for, it was wrong—putting things in or letting words out.

"I'll go ride my bike," he announced. When Marcus and Marius woke up from their naps, they were pretty cranky. It would be better to stay outside.

"Good," said Mrs. Cott.

"I have to ride by Cricket's house," he said. Lucas didn't want to wait until tomorrow to tell her that for once she had gotten an answer wrong. She didn't even know what the word *obstreperous* meant. Boy, was she dumb.

2

EYEGLASSES

Breakfast was always noisy and messy at Lucas's house. The twins, Marcus and Marius, were learning to feed themselves, so there were usually drops of oatmeal or pieces of toast falling on the floor. Sometimes Marcus would throw a section of orange to Marius. Sometimes Marius would stick his hand into the bowl of cereal and then rub it in his hair.

Mr. Cott had to leave the house very early each morning to get to work. Mrs. Cott was kept busy as she ran from one twin to the other trying

14

to keep order and see that most of the breakfast ended up inside their stomachs.

As Lucas was getting ready to leave for school, his mother said, "I'm going to make an appointment for your father and me to speak with Mrs. Hockaday. I want to tell her that you are going to try and turn over a new leaf."

Lucas looked puzzled. He had already promised to behave. What was this business about a leaf? Mrs. Cott saw that her son didn't understand.

"A new leaf means that you will begin all over. You will try to be the perfect student in Mrs. Hockaday's class."

As he walked toward school, Lucas thought about what his mother had said. Being perfect didn't sound like much fun. But he would give it a try.

The first thing Lucas noticed when he came into class was that Arthur Lewis was wearing a brand-new pair of eyeglasses. Arthur was a quiet boy, and he rarely spoke out in class. But with his new glasses he looked very important and very smart. He looked smarter than Cricket Kaufman, and he looked as if he knew that the glasses had given him a new power. Arthur surprised everyone that morning by raising his hand and answering two of Mrs. Hockaday's questions. He had never done that before.

Lucas turned around to look at Arthur. He wished that he had glasses with dark frames like that. It would be easier to behave if he were wearing eyeglasses. At lunchtime, Lucas asked Arthur if he could try them on.

Arthur refused. "My mother said that glasses are not toys. She said that I should leave them on and not take them off."

"You could take them off for a minute to rest your eyes while you're eating," suggested Lucas. "That isn't playing with your glasses."

Arthur considered Lucas's suggestion. Then he said, "No. I'm not taking my glasses off. If you want glasses then you have to get your own."

Lucas looked around the room. Six or seven other children in other classes were also wearing glasses. Lucas had never noticed them before.

Lucas decided that if he wore glasses, he would definitely act differently. With glasses he would be a more serious student. He would not shout out in class or act in an obstreperous manner. He would be the perfect student. So after lunch, when he returned to the classroom, he raised his hand and told Mrs. Hockaday that he couldn't see the words she was writing on the chalkboard.

"Bring your paper and come sit up here," said Mrs. Hockaday, and she pointed to a seat that was empty because Sara Jane Cushman was absent.

Lucas walked slowly to the front of the room, bumping into several desks along the way.

"Are you drunk?" asked Julio.

"I can't see well," Lucas complained. "I think I need eyeglasses."

Sitting in the front seat wasn't much fun. None of his usual tricks like rolling the pencil were possible when he was sitting right in front of Mrs. Hockaday. But Lucas thought it would be worth the inconvenience if he could arrange to get glasses. He kept squinting his eyes whenever he remembered.

Mrs. Hockaday went over to Lucas. "I think you had better go to the nurse," she said.

Lucas sat up straighter. "Yes, Mrs. Hockaday," he agreed.

"Ask her to examine your eyes. Perhaps you have strained them by watching too much TV," said the teacher.

"Watching TV doesn't strain my eyes," said Lucas quickly. He hoped he hadn't planted any weird ideas in Mrs. Hockaday's head.

The nurse's office was at the end of the hall. When he got there, Lucas saw Mrs. Phillips, the nurse, taking the temperature of Carol Simmons, who was in one of the other third grade classes. Carol was lying on the cot in the nurse's office and her face was all flushed.

"What can I do for you, Lucas?" asked Mrs. Phillips.

"Mrs. Hockaday said you should examine my eyes," he reported. Then he remembered to squint again.

Mrs. Phillips took the thermometer from Carol Simmons's mouth and studied it. "You are a shade over a hundred," she said. "Just lie here and rest until it's time to go home."

Then the nurse walked to the front of the room and pulled down the chart that was used for examining eyes. "Stand on that yellow line," she instructed Lucas. "Now cover your right eye with this piece of paper."

Lucas took the paper from the nurse and covered his eye. He could read all the letters on

the chart perfectly. However, he pretended that he couldn't.

Mrs. Phillips pointed to a line of letters.

"K-P-Z-X-M-T," Lucas read, although he could see quite well that the letters on the chart were none of those.

"Try the line above," said Mrs. Phillips.

Again Lucas gave only the wrong letters.

"Your eyes certainly seem to have changed since the last time they were examined," said Mrs. Phillips. "Try the other eye."

Lucas shifted the paper to cover his left eye. Once again he read out letters that he did not see but that he hoped would convince the nurse that he badly needed eyeglasses.

Carol Simmons sat up on the cot and watched.

"Are you going blind?" she asked Lucas.

Lucas smiled proudly. "I guess I need glasses like Arthur Lewis," he informed Carol and the nurse.

"I will write a note to your mother to take you to an eye doctor," said Mrs. Phillips, and she went over to her desk.

"I'm sorry about your eyes," said Carol.

"That's okay," said Lucas. "I'm going to get glasses now."

"Yeah, but I remember last year you said you wanted to be an astronaut."

"This year I want to be a wrestler," Lucas said.

"That's good because you need twenty-twenty vision to be an astronaut," Carol told Lucas.

"I never knew that," he said.

"I heard it on a TV program," said Carol.

"Can't you be an astronaut if you wear eyeglasses?" Lucas asked Mrs. Phillips. He might want to change back to being an astronaut instead of a wrestler. Then what?

"I really don't know," said the nurse. "But don't worry. There are so many things you can do when you grow up. The important thing is that glasses will enable you to see better. Your eyesight seems to be deteriorating rapidly. I never saw such a change. It should be looked into by a doctor at once."

Carol Simmons lay back on the cot. "No one would want to be in a spaceship flown by a blind astronaut," she said.

"I'm not blind," said Lucas. "I can see perfectly."

He put the little paper in front of his right eye again. "T-R-N-K-O-P," he read from the very bottom line. "I can even see what it says on the very, very bottom of the chart. 'Printed in Topeka, Kansas. 1982.' "

Lucas turned to face Carol Simmons. "See, I told you I'm not blind."

"Lucas Cott, what is this all about?" asked Mrs. Phillips. "I don't have time to play games with you!"

"I recovered," said Lucas. "Thanks for the eye checkup," he said.

"You should never believe anything Lucas Cott says," said Carol Simmons. "I was in his class last year. I know all about him."

"I know all about you, too," said Lucas.

"What do you know?" Carol demanded.

"I'm not telling," said Lucas.

"But I'm telling you to go back to your classroom at once," Mrs. Phillips scolded Lucas. "And don't try any of your nonsense with me in the future."

"What did Mrs. Phillips say about your

22

eyes?" Julio asked Lucas when he returned to his seat.

"I'm not telling," said Lucas. And he began to copy all the sentences from the chalkboard. He could see every one of them perfectly.

3

TURNING OVER
A NEW LEAF

H ere is a homework assignment for tomorrow," said Mrs. Hockaday.

Everyone groaned. The loudest protest came from Lucas. He hated homework. Lots of times he didn't even bother to do it. Instead he made up excuses about why his homework had not been done.

"It's a lovely autumn day outside," said their teacher. "So I want you each to bring one or two leaves that you find on the ground. Tomorrow we will identify them. There are many types of trees around here. It will be interesting to see what you find."

Cricket Kaufman raised her hand. "Don't you want us to write a report about our leaves as part of our homework?" she asked.

Lucas looked across the aisle at Cricket. He wished he had a spitball handy. What sort of stupid question was that?

Luckily, Mrs. Hockaday did not decide to have the third graders write reports. "Just leaves," she said, smiling. "But there is no excuse for anyone forgetting to bring them tomorrow. That means you, too, Lucas," she added. Lucas had become quite famous in class for not remembering to do his homework.

"I'll bring the most leaves of anyone," said Lucas. "See if I don't." He had suddenly remembered his promise to his mother. If he was going to turn over a new leaf, then he had to do his homework. The funny thing was that he was expected to bring an old leaf into class.

On the way home, Lucas noticed several of his classmates picking up leaves. He didn't bother. He had helped his father rake leaves in their backyard over the weekend. He knew there were several huge plastic bags full of leaves sitting in front of their house waiting for the garbage pickup the next day. Lucas thought he would just open one of the bags and take out a handful of leaves.

When he got home and looked at the bags, Lucas got an idea. Wouldn't it be funny if he brought a whole bag of leaves into his class tomorrow. He had told Mrs. Hockaday that he would bring more leaves than anyone else. And it would certainly be worth the effort just to see the expression on Cricket Kaufman's face. Lucas tried to lift one of the bags but it was too heavy to carry all the way to school.

In the garage, Lucas had an old wagon that he used to play with when he was little. It would be perfect for hauling the bag of leaves to school the next day. He decided not to tell his parents about his plan. His mother would probably say that he didn't have to bring so many leaves to school. But she hadn't heard the tone that Mrs. Hockaday used when she said "That means you, too, Lucas." Tomorrow he would show Mrs. Hockaday that he could do homework better than anyone else, if he wanted to.

The next morning, Lucas took his lunch box

and put it in the wagon. Then he lifted one of the huge bags of leaves and put it in the wagon, too. He had to pull the wagon slowly so the bag didn't fall off.

"Where are you taking that bag?" asked the crossing guard.

"It's my homework," said Lucas proudly.

The crossing guard looked very surprised.

At the entrance to the school there were several steps. Lucas would never have managed to get the wagon with the heavy bag of leaves up to the top if a couple of big sixth grade boys hadn't been standing nearby.

"Will you help me?" he asked them.

They didn't question the wagon or its load. They just lifted the whole thing up to the top of the steps for Lucas.

"Thanks," he called to them as he slowly pulled his wagon down the school corridor.

Mrs. Hockaday was sitting at her desk writing in her plan book. "You're early this morning," she said to Lucas when she looked up and saw him entering the room. Then Mrs. Hockaday noticed that Lucas was pulling a wagon behind him and on the wagon was a huge plastic bag.

"What in the world is that?" she asked.

"It's my homework," said Lucas. "I told you I would bring more leaves than anyone else."

"You mean you brought that whole bag filled with leaves?" gasped Mrs. Hockaday. Lucas was unpredictable, but today he seemed to have outdone himself.

"Yes," said Lucas, nodding his head and smiling. "Where should I put them? They won't fit in my desk."

"Just leave the wagon in the corner," said the teacher.

Lucas pulled the wagon to the corner of the room. Then he lifted up the bottom of the plastic bag to get his lunch box. As he removed the box, it tore a large hole in the side of the plastic bag and a pile of leaves fell on the floor. Just then the bell rang and the rest of his class came into the room. There was a draft from the hallway and some of the leaves began to blow around the room.

Lucas tried to catch them. He didn't want his homework flying all over. The other boys and girls rushed about trying to grab at the leaves, too. More leaves fell from the bag and soon the room was filled with leaves.

"It's fall in our classroom," cried Lucas.

"We are going to need a rake to clean up this mess," said Cricket.

Mrs. Hockaday slammed the classroom door shut. She only did that when she was very angry. "Everyone in your seats!" she shouted. She looked at the mess in the room. "Cricket, will you please go and find the custodian. He will help us sweep up the room."

Cricket rushed out of the classroom. As she opened the door, still more leaves swirled through the air. Lucas stood on his desk and tried to catch a leaf that was flying overhead.

"Lucas, get down at once!" shouted Mrs. Hockaday. "I have enough to think about without you breaking your head."

Lucas sat down. There were several leaves on his desk and many, many more on the floor. The custodian arrived carrying a large broom and a plastic bag of his own. He began sweeping up the leaves from between the desks and the corners of the room. Whenever he missed a leaf, a student would call it to his attention. It took quite a while but eventually all the leaves were swept up and put into the custodian's plastic bag, which did not have a hole in it.

"At last we can begin our work," said Mrs.

Hockaday when the custodian and the broom and the plastic bag and the leaves were gone from the classroom.

"When are you going to look at our leaves?" asked Cricket Kaufman, holding up two bright red leaves that she had brought for her homework.

"Later. Much later," said Mrs. Hockaday with a sigh.

Suddenly, Lucas felt a sinking feeling in his stomach. His leaves had all been swept away. He didn't have anything to show for his homework. All his efforts had been for nothing. One minute he had more leaves than anyone else in the class and the next minute he didn't have even a single one.

But then he noticed something sticking out from underneath his foot on the floor. There was one leaf that the custodian had missed. It was small and yellow. Lucas picked it up and put it inside his social studies book so that it wouldn't get lost. Now no one could say that he hadn't done his homework.

Today Mrs. Hockaday couldn't even say that he had been obstreperous.

4

<table>
<tr><td>

LUCAS MAKES
A BET

</td></tr>
</table>

One Thursday in November, Cricket Kaufman came rushing into the classroom all excited. "My mother had our baby," she announced very proudly to everyone.

"That's wonderful," said Mrs. Hockaday. "Is it a girl or a boy?"

"It's a girl baby," said Cricket. "And her name is Monica. My father says she looks just like me."

"How come they didn't name her after a bug like you?" asked Lucas. There were lots of names that he could think of: Mosquito Kaufman, Ladybug Kaufman, or Cockroach Kaufman.

Mrs. Hockaday ignored Lucas's comment. But Cricket surprised him by turning angrily and saying, "Oh yeah, well how come your parents didn't name you Mucus, to go with the names of your brothers—Marcus, Marius, and Mucus."

"Mucus!" Julio shouted. "Mucus Cott!"

"Julio. Stop that at once! You, too, Lucas. And I'm surprised at you, Cricket. You mustn't let Lucas's teasing make you so upset. If your sister grows up to be just like you, it will be a pleasure to have her in my class someday. But calling out is not proper behavior from anyone." She looked at Lucas and Julio sternly. "Is that understood?"

Lucas remembered that he had promised his mother he wasn't going to call out in class. But once again, he seemed to have forgotten. It seemed as if the words were always flying out of his mouth before he could remember to keep still. So now, even though he was furious at what Cricket had said, he kept quiet. He waited until they were walking out of class at the end of the day to tell her something he bet she didn't know.

"My name is Roman," he said. "And Marcus and Marius have Roman names, too. That's because my grandparents came from Italy, and in the olden days Rome was the most important place in the world."

"Well, that doesn't make you so important now," said Cricket. "You think you are so special because you have twins at your house. I bet my sister is going to be smarter than your brothers. And she's prettier, too."

"Don't you say anything against my brothers. They're better than your baby sister any day," said Lucas angrily.

"You haven't even seen my sister," said Cricket, sticking her tongue out at Lucas.

"You'll see," said Lucas knowingly. "Babies aren't all that great. They make a lot of noise and they smell, too. And they take up a lot of your parents' time. At least Marcus and Marius are two years old; they can learn things from me."

"If you are teaching them to be just like you then they're going to get into trouble all the time, just like you."

"Oh yeah?"

"Yeah. You couldn't keep quiet if your life depended on it," Cricket said to Lucas. "Your mouth is open all day long. I'm surprised you don't wake yourself up talking in your sleep."

"Listen," said Lucas. "Mouths are meant for talking. And eating," he added, licking his lips.

"You don't eat all day, and you shouldn't talk all day, either," said Cricket. "Poor Mrs. Hockaday has to listen to you talking constantly."

"I don't talk that much," said Lucas, defending himself. "And besides, if I wanted to, I could stop talking. It's just that I have a lot to say."

"I bet you couldn't keep quiet for more than two seconds."

"Want to bet?" asked Lucas.

"Sure," said Cricket.

"What do you want to bet?" asked Lucas.

"My grandma gave me a dollar last night because I was such a big girl with my new baby sister. I'll bet you that dollar that you couldn't go through a day at school without saying a single word."

"You're on," said Lucas. "Tomorrow my lips will be sealed."

"Okay. But if you talk at all, if you say one

single word in school tomorrow, then you have to give *me* a dollar," warned Cricket.

"No sweat," said Lucas. He didn't have a dollar to pay her, but he had no intention of losing the bet. It would be an easy way to earn a dollar, and he would show Cricket Kaufman that she didn't know everything. He could be quiet if he wanted to. He just never had wanted to before. And after he won the bet, he would talk twice as much the next day to get her really annoyed. It was a great plan.

The next morning, Lucas left home and started off to school. He wasn't sure at which point the bet began. Could he speak in the school yard? What about during recess and lunchtime? No matter. He wouldn't say a word all day. There was no way that he was going to lose this bet.

"Hi, Lucas," Cricket called out as she saw him approaching.

Lucas nodded to her but he did not say anything.

"Don't forget," said Cricket. "One word and you owe me a dollar."

Lucas nodded his head in agreement and went into the classroom. There was no sense in standing around outside if he couldn't speak to anyone.

After a few minutes the bell rang and all the students filed into the classroom. Mrs. Hockaday came in and sat down at her desk. At the beginning of the school year, she had called the attendance each morning. But now that she knew all her students, she merely looked around the room and could spot who was absent.

"One hundred percent attendance," she said, looking up and down the rows. "That's a fine way to end the week."

Lucas was just about to call out that the best way to end the week was to go home, when he remembered that he was not going to speak. He pressed his lips together and took out his arithmetic workbook. He paid close attention to everything that Mrs. Hockaday wrote on the chalkboard, and he shook his head when Julio poked him to say something.

"What's the matter?" whispered Julio, noticing the way Lucas was keeping his lips pressed together. "You feel like throwing up or something?"

Lucas shook his head and kept writing in his

workbook. He wanted to tell Julio that school always made him feel sick, but he knew he couldn't even whisper without Cricket hearing him. He looked in her direction and saw that she was watching him closely.

"Cricket? Why aren't you doing your problems?" Mrs. Hockaday called out.

"I'm finished already," Cricket replied proudly.

"Well, go over them again," said the teacher. "We don't want any careless errors."

Cricket pretended to go over her arithmetic, but Lucas could see that she was still watching him. This was going to be a long day.

During social studies, Mrs. Hockaday asked the class which explorer discovered the Pacific Ocean. Lucas knew the answer but he did not raise his hand. He listened as the students tried to guess the answer.

"Columbus," said Julio.

"Marco Polo," said Sara Jane.

Cricket was waving her hand frantically. "I know. I know," she called out.

"Of course you know, Cricket," said Mrs. Hockaday, smiling at her star student. "But I want some of the other students to try and remember. We talked about this man yesterday. Here is a clue: his name starts with a *B*."

No one seemed to know the answer except Cricket and Lucas. But Lucas couldn't say it without losing the bet and Mrs. Hockaday didn't want to call on Cricket. She had already answered the last five questions that the teacher asked.

"Open your books to page seventy-two," Mrs. Hockaday instructed the class.

Everyone did.

"Now, Lucas, please start reading from the top of the page. You will find the answer to the question there."

Lucas froze. He looked over at Cricket. Did reading count as speaking? It had been stupid of him not to make the rules for this bet clear before he agreed to it.

Cricket was grinning from ear to ear. It was obvious to Lucas that she thought he would have to pay her a dollar if he read aloud in class. Lucas sat staring at page seventy-two, but he did not begin reading.

"Lucas," said Mrs. Hockaday, "we're all waiting."

Lucas thought fast. He began to cough.

Then he doubled up and coughed into his hands.

"You had better get yourself a drink of water," Mrs. Hockaday said. "Julio, would you read from the top of page seventy-two?"

Lucas dashed out into the hall. He was lucky to have gotten out of that situation. He hoped he could keep it up through the rest of the day. He took a long, slow drink of water at the fountain and went back into the classroom.

"So now we all know who discovered the Pacific Ocean," Mrs. Hockaday was saying as he entered the classroom. "Lucas, do you know?" she asked.

Lucas stopped midway to his seat. He nodded his head and smiled at the teacher.

"Who was it?" asked Mrs. Hockaday.

Lucas was about to double up in a second coughing fit. However, he suddenly realized that he had another alternative. He walked to the front of the room and picked up a piece of chalk. BALBOA, he wrote on the chalkboard in huge letters.

"Excellent," said Mrs. Hockaday. "I'm glad to see that you know how to spell the name."

Lucas returned to his seat, smiling at Cricket as he passed her desk.

Lunch was hard. But it could have been harder. Lucas chewed his sandwich very, very slowly. He took teeny-tiny bites and teeny-tiny sips from his container of milk.

"What's the matter? Are you mad at me?" Julio asked.

Lucas smiled his friendliest smile but didn't answer. He pointed to his sandwich and then took another bite.

"You've gone bananas," said Julio.

Lucas wanted to ask how you could go bananas while eating a tuna fish sandwich, but he resisted the temptation. Tomorrow when he had his prize dollar from Cricket he would buy Julio a candy bar or a pack of gum.

USSR was easy. Lucas read his book while his classmates read theirs. Some days he found it hard to keep still for fifteen whole minutes. His classmates seemed to expect him to create some sort of diversion. But today all he did was read. Lucas got so involved in the story he was reading that he was sorry when the quiet time ended. He decided that he would take the book home for the weekend, instead of leaving it in his desk. He wanted to find out what happened next.

Lucas realized that he was lucky this was Friday. On Thursdays his class had music. How would he have avoided singing with the others? Cricket would have said that singing was talking to music. On Friday, the class had no music, no gym, no art. It was always a long and boring day, but today's challenge made it seem longer than ever.

"I have a treat for you all," said Mrs. Hockaday.

The students looked at her with surprise. "Since Cricket has just gotten a new baby in her family, I stopped by the public library yesterday and borrowed a film about babies. I think you will all find it interesting."

Lucas opened his mouth to ask, "Does it tell us where they come from?" But before he could say a word, he caught Cricket looking triumphant. He had almost lost the bet. He closed his mouth tightly.

Mrs. Hockaday wheeled a projector out of the closet. The film was already set up. She asked Arthur to turn out the lights, and she began to show the film. It was funny to see the little babies eating and slopping food all over. It reminded Lucas of his brothers at home. When the babies' diapers were being changed, there were a few whistles and calls from some of the boys. But Lucas did not make a sound. He wondered if Cricket could see him in the dark. He didn't want her to accuse him of making noises.

The film ended and it was time to get ready to go home. Mrs. Hockaday walked over to Lucas. "You've been very quiet all day," she said. "Do you feel all right?" She put her hand on his forehead.

Lucas blushed. On any other day he would have made a remark to the teacher, but now he kept silent.

"You may be coming down with something," said Mrs. Hockaday. "Get to bed early tonight and drink a lot of orange juice. I don't want you to get sick and have to miss school."

Lucas was surprised by his teacher's comment. He would have thought she would be glad if he was absent. Maybe she did like him, after all.

"I noticed that he's sick," said Julio. "He's been acting weird all day long."

The bell rang and Mrs. Hockaday dismissed the class.

"I can't believe you really kept quiet all day," said Cricket as she and Lucas walked out the door.

"You're not going to trick me into talking," said Lucas. "Wait till we get outside."

"I tricked you already!" shouted Cricket. "I fooled you, Lucas Cott. You kept quiet the whole day but you didn't wait until you got out of school. You owe me a dollar bill."

"I do not!" Lucas shouted at her.

"You do so."

"The bell rang. School is over even if we are still inside it. You said I couldn't keep quiet all day long at school and I did. You owe me a dollar," Lucas said.

"Lucas," said Mrs. Hockaday, coming out into the hallway. "It looks to me like you are making a fine recovery without orange juice. I guess you had a case of too much school. Go home now and enjoy the weekend."

Cricket ran ahead of Lucas and kept running all the way out of the building and into the street. Lucas had a feeling that he wasn't going to get the dollar that he had won. But he also knew that there was no way that Cricket could ever make him pay her a penny.

As he walked home, Lucas thought about all that had happened during the day. He remembered how concerned Mrs. Hockaday had sounded when she thought he was getting sick. He wasn't going to have another bet with Cricket, but maybe he wouldn't call out so much either. He liked it when Mrs. Hockaday liked him. It was a nice feeling.

5

WRESTLING FEATS

E ven though Marcus and Marius were only two years old, it was hard for Lucas to remember before they were born. It was almost as if his memory began the morning he was awakened by his father and given the big news. The baby brother or baby sister that they had been expecting had turned out to be twin boys. It had been a surprise for everyone: Lucas, his parents, and even the doctor who had delivered the babies.

Life at the Cott house had not been the same since!

At first it had been loads of fun for Lucas. There was a lot of company at the house and many people had brought him presents. It was as if he had done something quite clever by having two new baby brothers at one time.

Then, when the novelty wore off, it became less pleasant. The twins cried a lot, and when they weren't crying they were eating. Because there were two of them, it took both parents to feed them. "If only I could buy another pair of arms," Mrs. Cott would sigh as both Marcus and Marius began howling at the same time. Lucas offered to help, but although he was a big brother, he was still considered too small to carry a crying baby around the house.

Now that they were two years old, Lucas found his brothers more fun. He enjoyed watching them climb all over everything. They got into more mischief than he could ever have thought of. And because there were two of them, if one was taking all the pots and groceries out of the kitchen cupboards, the other one might be throwing toys or clothes down the toilet.

Lucas thought his brothers were very funny, except for the time Marius tore the labels off all the canned goods and they couldn't figure out which were tomatoes and which were peaches when it was suppertime. It also wasn't funny when Marcus stopped up the toilet on a Saturday night, and the plumber couldn't be reached until Monday morning.

But by and large, Lucas knew that having two such good mischief-makers around the house made his life easier. His parents were so preoccupied with Marcus and Marius that they didn't have time to worry about him, too. The note from Mrs. Hockaday was the perfect example. If Lucas had been an only child, Mrs. Cott would certainly have been more upset. Julio had told Lucas that the time the teacher sent a note home to his parents, he had been grounded for a week. He wasn't allowed to ride his bike or watch TV or anything.

Lucas had not been punished at all. Instead, he had a long talk with his father. As they walked around the block, Lucas discovered that Mrs. Hockaday had told his parents that he was one of the brightest students in the class.

"She doesn't treat me like I'm smart," complained Lucas.

"And you don't act very smart in her classroom," his father said. "But she sees your potential."

Lucas had promised to try harder to behave himself at school.

It wasn't easy, so he was very glad when the weekend arrived and he could relax at home. Often on Saturday, Julio would come over on his bike. Or Lucas went over to Julio's. But there were times when he discovered that he enjoyed playing with his little brothers just as much as he liked playing with his friends.

For one thing, ever since he had begun watching wrestling matches on television and decided that he wanted to become a wrestler, he had two in-house opponents on which to practice his holds.

Lucas was learning them all. There was the half nelson, the figure four, the cradle, and the switch. And there were many others, too. Lucas was careful not to hurt his brothers. He only wrestled with them on the living room floor where there was a thick carpet to ease their falls. Both Marcus and Marius enjoyed playing with their big brother. When he pulled them down and pinned them to the floor, they would crow with delight. Lucas noticed that they in turn practiced the holds on each other.

Lucas liked to have a daily scrimmage with his brothers. One Saturday morning, Lucas was just in the midst of perfecting a new hold called a double chicken wing on Marcus when his mother came into the living room.

"Oh, Lucas," she sighed. "Are you wrestling with Marcus again? One of these days you're going to hurt him."

"No one gets hurt in the wrestling matches on TV," Lucas said. "Dad said all those groans that the wrestlers make are just for show. Don't worry. I won't hurt Marcus or Marius."

"You may not hurt them on purpose," Mrs. Cott said. "But they are so small, you could break an arm or a leg accidentally. Can't you think of a different game to play with them?"

"More, more," Marcus demanded, pushing at Lucas.

"See, he likes it," Lucas defended himself. "I'm careful with them. And besides, if I want to be a wrestler, I have to practice."

Mrs. Cott sighed. "Maybe it's time to change to another field. Let's see. So far you've decided to be a fire fighter, a police officer, an astronaut, and a wrestler. How about something quiet and peaceful. Did you ever think of becoming a poet?"

Lucas sat on the living room floor and considered this new option. "I have two brothers who are twins ..." he began. "Twins, swins, pins, grins ...

"I have two brothers who are twins,
They are always full of grins.
When I throw them on the floor,
They always shout for more."

"See, you have a natural aptitude," said Mrs. Cott.

Lucas reached over to Marcus, who was tearing the pages out of a magazine he had found on the coffee table. "I can be the wrestling poet," he said. "All the wrestlers on TV have a gimmick."

Mr. Cott came into the living room carrying Marius. Marius had smeared lipstick all over his face. "I thought you'd like to see this before I wash him up," he told his wife.

"Oh, no," gasped Mrs. Cott. "What does

the bedroom look like? And how did he reach my lipstick anyhow?"

"The bedroom is just fine," Lucas's father reassured her. "He was so busy decorating himself that he forgot about his surroundings."

"Thank goodness for small favors," sighed Mrs. Cott as her husband took Marius off to the bathroom.

Lucas pulled up his shirt sleeve. "Hey, Dad," he said. "Look at my muscles. They're getting bigger and bigger now that I'm in training for wrestling."

Mr. Cott squeezed the muscle in Lucas's arm. "Great! This winter you'll be strong enough to help shovel the snow for us," he told his son. Lucas grinned proudly.

Lunch was tomato vegetable soup. It tasted good but the twins slopped more of it under the table than into their mouths.

"I have a wonderful idea," said Mrs. Cott. Lucas looked at her hopefully. "The boys all need haircuts," she said. "Lucas's hair is in his eyes and the twins need a good trim, too. Let's all go to the barbershop this afternoon."

It wasn't Lucas's idea of a wonderful idea at

all, but at least it would be more fun if the whole family went.

"All right," agreed Mr. Cott. "I could use a haircut myself."

So they all got into the car and drove to the barbershop. Lucas had been getting his hair cut at the same barbershop ever since he was a small boy. He liked to watch the three barbers at their work. He always wondered if they trimmed one another's hair at times when there were no customers waiting on the chairs that were lined up against the wall.

"No, no," said Marius when he recognized where they were going. He didn't like haircuts.

"It's fun, Marius," Lucas lied to his brother.

"No fun," Marius said.

"I'll get my hair cut first," suggested Lucas. "Then you can watch and see that it doesn't hurt at all."

A barber named Louie finished trimming the hair of a man who was mostly bald. Lucas wondered what it felt like to be bald. His favorite wrestler was Hairless Harry, who was so bald that his scalp shone on the television screen.

"I like the way Louie cuts my hair," Mr.

Cott whispered to the others. "If you don't mind, I'll go first."

"Sure," said Mrs. Cott. "Then you'll be able to give me a hand when the twins get their haircuts."

"You don't need any help from me," said Lucas's father. "That's what the barbers are for."

"That's what you think," said Mrs. Cott. "This is the first time you ever came to the barbershop with the boys."

Mr. Cott looked at Marius and Marcus. They had gotten off their chairs and were making little piles out of the hair on the floor.

"Next," called Louie. He looked very pleased when Mr. Cott got onto his chair.

The other two barbers kept looking up from their work to see how far along the other was. One of them would avoid cutting the twins' hair if he worked slowly enough and Louie finished cutting Mr. Cott's hair. Finally, the barber named Tony finished working on his customer. He looked anxiously at Mrs. Cott as he said, "Next."

"It's my turn," said Lucas as he got onto the barber's chair. Tony smiled at him with delight.

"I like to cut big boys' hair," he said as he began snipping away. He worked so well that he forgot to stall. Lucas's hair was finished while Louie was still cutting Mr. Cott's hair.

"Next," said Tony. He looked across at the third barber. He was cutting one hair at a time.

"All right, Marcus. It's your turn," said Mrs. Cott.

Marcus looked up from the floor where he was still sitting. "No haircut," he said.

"It's fun," said Lucas. "I just had mine cut. Now it's your turn."

"Go ahead, Marcus," called Mr. Cott from under a damp towel which the barber had placed over his face.

"No," Marcus howled.

"No," Marius howled, too.

Mrs. Cott lifted Marcus up and put him onto the special seat that Tony had put on top of his chair. It had a steering wheel and was meant to look like a car.

"No. No. No!" howled Marcus, and he kept shaking his head so much that Tony was afraid to come near him with the scissors.

"I don't want to cut your boy," he explained to Lucas's mother.

"That's all right," said Mrs. Cott. "He'll settle down in a minute."

"No. No. No!" screamed Marcus. From the floor came an echoing howl from Marius.

"Come back next week," said Tony. "Not today."

"No, we're here now and you're not busy either," said Mrs. Cott.

"I can't cut the hair of a boy who jumps so much," said Tony.

"Wait," said Lucas. "I'll help you."

Lucas went over to Tony's chair and locked his arm around Marcus's neck and shoulder. He pressed his brother against the chair in the best headlock he had ever done. "Okay. Cut away," he instructed Tony.

The barber waited a moment to see if the little boy was going to break out of the hold. But Marcus didn't resist. He stayed still the way he always did when Lucas wrestled with him at home.

"I think this will work," said Tony, nodding his head, and quickly he began to cut.

"See, it's fun," Lucas insisted as he held Marcus in place. Some of Marcus's hair fell onto Lucas's face as the barber cut. But Lucas knew better than to let go of Marcus to wipe his face.

"My turn. My turn," Marius began to cry. He had been watching them.

"You're next," his mother promised him.

Tony worked fast. Soon Marcus's hair was quite short. Tony helped him down from the chair and picked up Marius. "Don't go away," he called to Lucas.

"Don't worry," said Lucas. "I know a lot of holds."

"My turn!" Marius shouted triumphantly.

Lucas reached behind the chair and shot his arms through his brother's. "This is the double chicken wing. I just learned how to do it this morning," he explained.

"It works well," said Tony, snipping away.

The third barber finished with his customer. He stood back and relaxed as he watched Tony cutting Marius's hair. Louie finished cutting Mr. Cott's hair, too.

Mr. Cott paid the bill for four haircuts. "See," he said to his wife. "There's nothing to it."

Mrs. Cott was busy brushing hairs off Marcus's pants.

"All done," said Tony, smiling. He turned to Lucas. "It's against the law to hire anyone so young," he said. "Otherwise, I would give you a job here real quick. You could hold all the little kids while I cut their hair. We'd make a good team."

"Maybe I'll come back when I'm older," said Lucas. "I never thought about becoming a barber before."

"You're not to practice by cutting your brothers' hair," Mrs. Cott warned Lucas as they walked out of the shop together.

"Why not?" asked Lucas. "You'd save a lot of money."

"Who wants ice-cream cones?" asked Mr. Cott as they walked past the ice-cream store, which was three doors down from the barber-shop.

"Me," shouted Marcus.

"Me," shouted Marius.

"Me," shouted Lucas.

"I wouldn't mind some," said Mrs. Cott.

They went inside and ordered their cones: strawberry for both of his parents, vanilla for the twins, and chocolate fudge ripple for Lucas. Lucas licked his cone and watched the man behind the counter as he scooped out the ice cream.

You needed good muscles to dig out the frozen ice cream from the deep bins. Maybe he wouldn't be a wrestler or a barber. Maybe he would use his new muscles to work in an ice-cream parlor. Life was filled with possibilities, he realized. Wouldn't Cricket Kaufman and Julio and all the other kids be surprised if they walked into the ice-cream store and he was working behind the counter?

6

THE CULTURAL
ARTS PROGRAM

One Friday afternoon, the Cultural Arts Committee of the PTA scheduled a mime to peform at the school. Lucas didn't even know what a mime was until his teacher explained it to the class.

"A mime is a performer who can tell a story by using his or her body and not saying a single word," Mrs. Hockaday said. "It will be a wonderful experience for you all."

"That's what she said last time," Lucas reminded Julio. Last time had been a month ago when the cultural arts program had been a coloratura soprano. She sang so loudly that it had hurt Lucas's ears, and no one understood a single song she sang because all the words were in foreign languages.

This time language wouldn't be a problem since the mime wasn't going to speak at all.

At one-thirty in the afternoon, the third graders marched into the multipurpose room. The lunch tables and chairs had been put away and everyone was to sit on the floor. First and second graders were in the front and the third graders had to sit in back. Lucas couldn't wait until next year when the fourth grade attended programs with the fifth and sixth grades. Then they would get the front row position again.

"Remember," warned Mrs. Hockaday, "I don't want to be embarrassed by bad behavior from anyone in this class. I don't want to hear a single sound out of any of you. There will be a big homework assignment over the weekend for anyone who speaks during the performance."

The threat worked. No one said a word as the class shifted about on the floor getting settled for the show. Lucas looked at Mrs. Hockaday sitting on one of the chairs along the side of the room. Teachers never had to sit on the floor.

In the back of the room was an empty chair with no one on it. Quietly, Lucas crept onto the chair.

Mrs. Hockaday saw him. Instead of calling his name, she snapped her fingers to get his attention, then gestured for him to get off the chair. He hadn't really expected to get away with it, but it didn't hurt to try, Lucas thought as he slid to the floor beside the empty chair.

Mr. Herbertson, the principal, came forward and called for attention. He told the students about the wonderful treat that was in store for them. He thanked Mrs. Weiss and Mrs. Corbett of the PTA and everyone clapped. Someone even whistled, but Mr. Herbertson gave him the evil eye and the whistling promptly stopped.

"And now, without further ado," said Mr. Herbertson, "Mr. Mime."

Lucas wondered what Mr. Mime's real name was. He wondered if he had legally changed his name. He couldn't have been born a mime.

Mr. Mime blew up an imaginary balloon. He blew it bigger and bigger. Everyone watched as he soundlessly puffed and puffed into the balloon. Then Mr. Mime tied an imaginary knot and attached a string to the balloon. Then the balloon began to lift Mr. Mime off the ground. That was stupid, thought Lucas. If he blew up the balloon, it would be filled with carbon dioxide, not helium. Carbon dioxide wasn't lighter than air. Didn't this guy know anything?

Lucas leaned against the chair as he watched. A lot of the little kids in the first grade were laughing, but he didn't think this show was so great. What was so cultural about blowing up a balloon?

The chair that Lucas was leaning against was made of heavy plastic with a cut-out section where the back folded into the seat. Lucas stuck his head through the hole and rested his chin on the chair's seat. It was a neat way to watch the show, he thought. He had his own private chin rest.

Suddenly, Lucas felt someone poking him on the shoulder. He turned his head and saw Mr. Herbertson standing over him. The principal didn't say a word but he gestured, just like the mime, and silently indicated he wanted Lucas to sit up properly.

Lucas tried to slide his head out of the hole.

But although his head had gone in without any difficulty, it didn't seem to fit through the hole now. It was almost as if his head had blown up like a balloon during the past few seconds. Lucas smiled up at the principal and pretended he didn't notice that he was getting the evil eye.

He turned his head again and pressed against the hole. No luck.

Mr. Herbertson tugged at Lucas's shoulder. Then he tried pushing Lucas's head through the hole. The principal's fingers pulled Lucas's hair, and it made Lucas want to cry out. Luckily, he remembered Mrs. Hockaday's warning in time. If he ever got his head out of the chair, he didn't want to spend the weekend doing a homework assignment.

Lucas noticed that several of his classmates were no longer watching the mime. They were looking at him. He tried to grin at them as if he enjoyed having the chair around his neck. If he could talk, he would have said it was a new style of necklace. Since he had been forbidden to speak, he just kept on grinning.

More and more kids were looking at him. Mrs. Hockaday was standing next to him now, too. Without looking up, Lucas could recognize her open-toed shoes and the smell of her perfume.

Suddenly, Lucas felt something cold being spread on his neck and face. It had a sweet scent, too. Mrs. Hockaday was putting cold cream on him. Maybe she thought it would act as a lubricant and help free him.

Mr. Herbertson pushed one way and Mrs. Hockaday pulled the other. It was a tug-of-war with Lucas in the middle. He closed his eyes and wondered if this was a dream. Once, he dreamed he was drowning in a sea of lemon meringue. But he had used the breaststroke and had·managed to come up to the surface of the lemon meringue. Then he woke up. This time, he couldn't seem to wake up.

Finally, Lucas felt the plastic rub against his ears as the chair came off over his head. He wasn't dreaming, but he was no longer a prisoner of the chair either. There was a huge burst of applause and the whistler at the other end of the room let out a few loud blasts as well. Lucas stood up and looked around.

Everyone in the room—first, second, and third graders, their teachers, the two PTA women from the Cultural Arts Committee, and even Mr.

Mime—were looking at him. Lucas thought he ought to bow in acknowledgment of all the applause. However, one glance at Mr. Herbertson made him think better of it.

Mrs. Hockaday turned to Mr. Mime and spoke. "I think this young man owes you an apology for interrupting your excellent performance," she said.

The mime didn't say a word. If he resented being upstaged by an eight-year-old, he didn't let anyone know. He came toward Lucas and took him by the hand. Then he gave Lucas one of his imaginary balloons. Lucas was no fool. He knew that he was in show business now. So he pretended that he was being lifted into the air, too. He stood on his tippy toes and then tried to grab hold of the mime for support. Together the two of them made their way to the front of the room. Everyone burst into applause again.

Lucas was ready for whatever the mime wanted to do next. He was not, however, prepared for Mrs. Hockaday, who also came forward. She took Lucas's arm and pulled him out the exit door.

"I have never been so frightened in my entire teaching career," she said to Lucas. "Suppose we couldn't get that chair off of your head? What would we have done? You could have been badly hurt!"

Lucas wasn't hurt. Everything was fine. But something in Mrs. Hockaday's tone stopped him from acting as if he didn't care. She cared. He could tell from the tone of her voice that she had really worried about him. She even looked like she was about to cry.

Later, when Lucas and all the rest of the students were back in their home room, Mrs. Hockaday's manner changed.

"Your behavior was terrible," she scolded Lucas. "You not only endangered yourself, but you were incredibly rude to the performer. The PTA especially arranged for that show, and you disrupted it with your foolish behavior. I'm assigning you fifty spelling words, each one to be written ten times."

Lucas didn't say anything. What could he say? The weekend was ruined. It would take forever to write all those spelling words over and over again and again.

Suddenly, Lucas saw a hand waving in the air. It was Cricket Kaufman. In recent weeks, since he had been controlling his tongue and not making comments about her in class, Cricket had been treating him better. Sometimes he almost thought he liked her. But what did she have to say now? Maybe she was going to suggest to the teacher that he should make up sentences with all those spelling words, too!

"Yes, Cricket," called Mrs. Hockaday.

"Mrs. Hockaday," said Cricket, "you never told us we couldn't put our heads through the chairs. I don't think it's fair for you to give Lucas a punishment for that. He didn't say a single word during the performance. And you only said you would punish anyone who spoke."

"Yes, yes," called out several of the other children in agreement.

Lucas stared at Cricket. She really sounded just like one of those lawyers on TV.

Mrs. Hockaday turned red. She had never ever scolded Cricket Kaufman. Lucas wondered if she was going to now.

Instead, she said, "Lucas, go to the bathroom and wash the cream off your face. And don't you ever, ever put your head through one of those chairs again. And that goes for everyone else in this classroom, too."

"Do I have to do the homework?" asked Lucas.

"Not this time," said Mrs. Hockaday.

Lucas's face broke into a huge smile. He looked over at Cricket. She wasn't so bad after all. Mrs. Hockaday wasn't so bad either, Lucas thought to himself as he washed his face in the boys' room.

He thought of how Cricket had come so unexpectedly to his defense. And at that moment, Lucas decided that he would vote for her when she ran for president of the United States. It was the very least he could do in return.

7

A CLASS CIRCUS
FOR A CLASS CLOWN

One afternoon in the spring, Mrs. Hockaday said, "It is time to start planning our class play for the assembly. I want everyone to put on their thinking caps."

It was a moment Lucas had been waiting for. Lately he had been behaving quite well in class. But sometimes, he just couldn't resist clowning around a bit. He had noticed that Mrs. Hockaday used the expression about thinking caps at least once every day of the year. So today he had brought his baseball cap from home, and when she told the students to put on their thinking caps, he pulled the blue cap from inside his desk where he had hidden it.

Everyone started to laugh.

"I wish I'd thought to bring my thinking cap from home, too," said Julio.

"I see our class clown is at it again," said Mrs. Hockaday. But for some reason, she didn't seem the least bit annoyed with Lucas. Maybe because he was behaving most of the time these days, she didn't mind if he did something silly once in a while.

Lucas grinned at his teacher.

"Now that you have your thinking cap on, see if you can come up with a good subject for our class play," said Mrs. Hockaday.

Lucas tried to think of something.

Arthur Lewis raised his hand. "My cousin's class did a play about famous people in history."

Lucas made a face. Arthur's suggestion didn't appeal to him. Why couldn't they do something that was fun, something that the class would like to do—and that the other students who would be the audience would like, too.

Famous people, Mrs. Hockaday wrote on the chalkboard. "Any other suggestions?"

"How about Cinderella?" asked Cricket Kaufman.

Lucas didn't think that was such a great idea either. He knew that Cricket was busy imagining herself in the starring role. But there weren't many good parts for boys in that story. Suddenly, Lucas had an idea.

"I know what," he called out.

"Lucas, don't call out. Raise your hand if you want to contribute something to our discussion," the teacher reminded him.

Lucas sighed and raised his hand. No matter how much he tried, he seemed to forget and call out at least once a day.

"Yes, Lucas, what do you think we should do?" asked Mrs. Hockaday.

"Let's put on a circus. Then everyone could do something different. And it would be lots of fun."

"Neat-o," shouted Julio.

"Don't call out," Mrs. Hockaday reminded him. But she could see from the reactions of the third graders that everyone liked the idea of presenting a circus.

"What do we need in a circus?" she asked.

Almost every hand in the class went up with

suggestions: clowns, acrobats, animals, a lion tamer.

"For once you can clown around all you want," said Mrs. Hockaday, smiling at Lucas as the parts were being assigned. "You and Julio can both be clowns in the play."

"I can do cartwheels," Julio offered. He had learned how to do them in phys ed, and he loved to show off his acrobatic skill in front of others.

"I have a unicycle that I got for Christmas," Franklin said. "Could I ride it?"

"That's an excellent suggestion," said Mrs. Hockaday. "You can be a clown, too."

"We will need someone to be the ringmaster," she went on. "The ringmaster is the person who will introduce all the acts. Arthur, I think that's a good job for you."

Everyone liked the idea of the circus. Only now that they had taken up his idea, Lucas was losing his enthusiasm for the project. He wasn't sure that he wanted to be a clown after all.

Why couldn't he have another part?

It was one thing to be a clown when you felt like it. It was quite another to be assigned to be a clown by your teacher. He didn't want to put red makeup on his nose like a clown. He would look silly, the way Marius looked when he had put his mother's lipstick all over his face.

The part in the circus that Lucas liked best was the part that had been given to Arthur Lewis. He wished he could be the ringmaster. He would wear a tall top hat and blow on a whistle to get everyone's attention. Then he would announce each act before it took place. It was an important part because there was only one ringmaster. Counting Franklin and Julio, there would be three clowns. And since Lucas didn't have a unicycle like Franklin, and he couldn't do cartwheels like Julio, Lucas knew that he wouldn't be a very good clown either.

"Our play is scheduled for May nineteenth," Mrs. Hockaday said as she wrote the date on the chalkboard. "We shall send written invitations to all your parents. I'm sure they will want to come and see you perform."

That was another reason Lucas wasn't looking forward to the class play. It was impossible for his parents to come to the show. His father's schedule did not permit him to take time off in the middle of the day. His mother couldn't leave

Marcus and Marius to come and watch him act. And he certainly didn't want his mother to bring the twins to school.

Last year, Lucas was one of the unsuccessful princes in the second grade's performance of *Sleeping Beauty*. Mrs. Cott had come to see the play, bringing both Marcus and Marius with her. At first, Lucas had been pleased to peek out from behind the curtain on the stage and see his mother and his two baby brothers. But during the second act, first Marius then Marcus began to cry, and Lucas was very embarrassed. Even when Mrs. Cott took the little boys out into the hallway outside the multipurpose room, the loud cries could be heard.

Cricket Kaufman had been playing the part of Sleeping Beauty. After the play was over, she told everyone that only a dead princess would have been able to sleep through all that racket.

"Your brothers ruined the play," she told Lucas at the time.

Of course, now she had a baby at home herself. Lucas wondered if Mrs. Kaufman was planning to bring their baby, Monica, to see the play. Lucas didn't care if Monica cried and ruined everything. He wasn't looking forward to the play at all.

In art, the children began to make the props for the play. Sara Jane Cushman's mother offered to help sew some simple costumes. Sara Jane was going to wear her ballet tights and her tutu and be a bareback rider on a cardboard elephant.

"This is the best play I was ever in," she told Mrs. Hockaday.

Lucas remembered that last year when Cricket had gotten the part of the Sleeping Beauty, Sara Jane had cried in class.

The next afternoon, Mrs. Hockaday neatly printed out the words of the official parent invitation on the chalkboard for everyone to copy:

**PLEASE PLAN TO ATTEND
THE THIRD GRADE MINICIRCUS
TO BE PRESENTED ON
THURSDAY, MAY 19, AT 1:30 P.M.
BY THE STUDENTS IN
MRS. HOCKADAY'S CLASS.**

Everyone copied the words onto special paper that Mrs. Hockaday distributed. Lucas felt like saying that every day was a circus in this class.

But he held his tongue. He didn't feel like making jokes. Everything connected with the play made him feel bad. When he was on stage with Julio and Franklin during rehearsals, he couldn't think of anything to do.

"Just be funny," said Julio. "You know. The way you always act."

"But I don't feel funny," Lucas said. And he just stood around and watched while Julio performed his cartwheels and walked on his hands and Franklin rode his unicycle around in circles.

"You must have stage fright," Mrs. Hockaday said. "All the best performers get stage fright before the show goes on. On the day of the class play, you will feel just fine."

Lucas knew he didn't have stage fright. When he had done funny things in the past, it was because he had wanted to. It was not much fun to be told to be funny. Lucas didn't like being a clown in the play and that's all there was to it.

He watched the other kids in the class as they rehearsed their parts. They were all enjoying themselves.

"Ladies and gentlemen," Arthur Lewis shouted, the way Mrs. Hockaday had instructed him. "Boys and girls. Welcome to the third grade circus."

"Minicircus. Don't forget to call it a minicircus," Mrs. Hockaday called out from the back of the room.

"Welcome to the minicircus," Arthur shouted.

"Third grade minicircus," Mrs. Hockaday corrected him.

Arthur blew his whistle and started again. Lucas sat and listened as Arthur rehearsed. He knew all the lines that the ringmaster had to say already, just from listening to Arthur repeating them so often.

That evening, Lucas gave his mother the invitation.

"This is lovely," she said, reading the message. "I remember your play from last year, but this sounds more original. What part do you have?"

"I'm a clown," said Lucas without much enthusiasm.

"That sounds like much more fun than a prince," said his mother, smiling at him as she grabbed hold of Marius, who was unrolling the paper towels. "This house is full of clowns. But

I'm sure you're the best."

"Do you have to bring Marcus and Marius?" Lucas asked. "They made so much noise last year, remember?"

"Yes." Mrs. Cott nodded. "They were noisy then, but they are older now. And I think they'll enjoy a circus more than *Sleeping Beauty.*"

"Well, if you want, you could stay home," Lucas suggested.

"Don't be silly. Of course I'll come," said Mrs. Cott. Lucas knew the twins would be obstreperous.

On the morning of May 19, something terrible happened. Mrs. Lewis phoned the school to report to Mrs. Hockaday that Arthur had developed tonsillitis. His throat was sore and he could not come to school.

Mrs. Hockaday walked up and down the front of the classroom in her open-toed shoes. "The show must go on," she informed the class. "But I don't know who can be the ringmaster on such short notice. Perhaps I'll have to do it myself."

Lucas started to shout out that he could do it. Just in time, he caught himself and raised his hand instead.

"Yes, Lucas, what do you want?" asked Mrs. Hockaday.

"Mrs. Hockaday, could I be the ringmaster? I know all the words."

"Lucas, you've had so much stage fright as a clown, how do you expect to take on an entirely new role?"

"Please," Lucas begged.

"I need you to be a clown with me," said Julio.

"Don't forget, I'm a clown, too," Franklin reminded Julio. "Two clowns are enough."

"Please," Lucas begged again.

"He could do it," Cricket said to reassure Mrs. Hockaday. "I bet he really knows the whole part."

Lucas looked across the aisle at Cricket. She smiled at him and he smiled back.

"If I let you be the ringmaster, you must be very serious about it," said the teacher. "You can't fool around. It is a very important part of the circus."

"I promise," said Lucas. He could imagine himself standing tall and blowing the whistle for everyone's attention. And he liked the top hat that Mrs. Cushman had made for Arthur.

"All right, Lucas." Mrs. Hockaday was smiling at him. "You have been trying very hard lately. Lucas, you are the new ringmaster."

The morning went by quickly because in addition to the regular work of arithmetic and social studies, they had to make get-well cards for Arthur. Mrs. Hockaday wrote the words on the chalkboard for them to copy:

DEAR ARTHUR,
I AM SORRY YOU ARE SICK. I MISS YOU AND I HOPE YOU WILL BE FEELING BETTER SOON.
                              YOUR CLASSMATE,

As Lucas printed out the words on his card, he thought about them. He was not the least bit sorry that Arthur was sick. It was the best thing that had happened to him in a long time. He did hope that Arthur would feel better soon. But not too soon. Suppose Arthur recovered by one-thirty this afternoon?

Arthur did not recover by one-thirty. After lunch, Mrs. Cushman arrived and helped Mrs. Hockaday to get the students into their costumes.

Julio loved the red makeup that he had on

his nose and cheeks. "Too bad the ringmaster doesn't get to wear any makeup," he told Lucas.

"That's okay," said Lucas. He was glad not to have to put paint on his face.

The third graders trooped down the hall to the multipurpose room. "Now don't be nervous," Mrs. Hockaday whispered to Lucas for the third time.

Lucas could see that his teacher was very nervous. All this time, he hadn't been the least bit nervous. But now, just before he was about to go up on the stage, his stomach felt a little funny. He was sorry that he had eaten all of his sandwich at lunchtime and half of Sara Jane's sandwich, too.

Suppose Mrs. Hockaday was right. Suppose he did have stage fright and forgot all of Arthur's lines. Everyone would laugh at him and it would be awful.

Something else bothered Lucas. He wondered if Marcus and Marius would call out when they recognized him. They might make a lot of noise and spoil the circus. Now that he was the ringmaster, he felt responsible for the success of the show. He worried that his brothers would ruin the third grade minicircus.

As the ringmaster, Lucas was the first to go on stage. He walked slowly across the platform and took a deep breath. Then he blew his whistle for attention. He paused and looked around at the audience. He saw his mother sitting off to one side with the other parents. To his surprise, his father was sitting next to her. But Lucas couldn't see any sign of Marcus and Marius. He wondered if they were already getting into mischief somewhere else in the room. He turned his head to look for them, but he couldn't see them anywhere.

"Lucas. Lucas! 'Ladies and gentlemen. Boys and girls. . . .' " hissed Mrs. Hockaday.

Lucas looked at his teacher, who was standing off to the side. He realized that she thought he had forgotten the words. In fact, he had been so busy worrying about his brothers that for a moment, he almost had. Then he remembered what Mrs. Hockaday had said: whatever happened, wherever his brothers were, the show must go on.

He smiled at the audience. Lucas was sure he knew every word of Arthur's part. He had heard it enough times. "Ladies and gentlemen. Boys and girls. Welcome to the third grade minicircus. ...." Lucas shouted, projecting his voice the way Mrs. Hockaday had instructed Arthur.

Soon Julio and Franklin were on stage. Julio did a series of cartwheels and handstands. Franklin rode around and around on his unicycle. In the background, there was music on the cassette player. It sounded just like a real circus.

Cricket came out in tights and a tutu and pretended she was walking across a tightrope. She was just like a mime, Lucas realized. Even though she was only walking across the floor, she really made you feel that she was high in the air and that she might lose her balance and fall at any moment. Lucas clapped very hard with the rest of the audience when she finished her part.

The circus proceeded just as they had planned it. Everyone remembered what to do and no one had stage fright. Lucas remembered every word of Arthur Lewis's part. At the end of the show, he proudly announced, "And now, my friends, all good things must come to an end. We hope you have enjoyed this third grade mini-circus."

The audience clapped loudly. Lucas knew it was one of the best school plays he had ever seen—even if he was in it himself. He was proud

that the idea of putting on a circus had been his.

All the parents came to the classroom to congratulate the students on their performance.

"Where are Marcus and Marius?" Lucas asked his mother.

"I arranged for Mrs. Williams to come and babysit with them this afternoon. They made so much noise last year, I decided not to risk disturbing your performance. But you weren't a clown. What happened?"

"You were great!" said Mr. Cott. "I'm glad I could arrange my schedule to get here."

"Wasn't he wonderful?" asked Mrs. Hockaday, putting her arm around Lucas and smiling at his parents. "He gave a surprise performance because our original ringmaster became ill. And what marvelous stage presence he had. He really amazed me. I wouldn't be surprised if Lucas decided to become an actor when he grows up. He has real talent."

Lucas looked at Mrs. Hockaday and thought about what she had just said. He had never considered becoming an actor before. It seemed much more interesting than being a wrestler. It was a new possibility for him to consider!

8

ANOTHER NOTE FROM MRS. HOCKADAY

The school year was ending. Ten months had passed since Lucas and his classmates had entered third grade. All the textbooks had been collected. All the drawings and papers that had been hanging around the room were taken down and distributed to the various artists and writers in the class.

On the last day of school, Julio leaned over and said to Lucas, "I made up a poem. Listen: 'Monday, Tuesday, Wednesday, Thursday, Friday, no more Hockaday.' What do you think of that?"

Lucas shrugged his shoulders. "Hockaday wasn't such a bad teacher," he said.

Just then Mrs. Hockaday came into the classroom carrying a large shopping bag. Everyone wondered what was in it.

"I am going to give out awards to the best students in this class," said Mrs. Hockaday.

Lucas sat up straight in his seat. Cricket Kaufman would certainly get an award. And Sara Jane Cushman would probably get a prize, too. Lucas wished he had known back in September that Mrs. Hockaday was going to give out prizes in June. Perhaps he would have tried harder right from the beginning. Lately, he hardly ever called out or did obstreperous things. But Mrs. Hockaday wouldn't forget how he behaved at the start of school. Teachers usually had good memories. Too good for the wrong things.

First, Mrs. Hockaday gave out report cards. The cards were yellow and on them Mrs. Hockaday had marked S for Satisfactory, U for Unsatisfactory, and I for Improvement Is Needed. Lucas looked at his report card. He had S for Conduct.

He had never gotten an S for Conduct before. Next to Reading, Spelling, Arithmetic, and Social Studies he had an S+. That was the best mark you could get. Lucas wondered if Cricket had gotten S+'s as well.

Also on the card was the name of the teacher he would have next year. Lucas had Mrs. Schraalenburgh. There was a joke in the school that only the smartest kids in fourth grade had Mrs. Schraalenburgh because no one else could either pronounce or spell her name. There were two other fourth grade teachers and Lucas knew that his class had been divided into three groups. Some would be together again with him in Mrs. Schraalenburgh's room, and the others would be in the other fourth grade classes.

There was a lot of whispering around the room because everyone wanted to know who else was going to be in their class. Mrs. Hockaday pretended that she didn't hear the whispering. Lucas had noticed that teachers scolded a lot on the first day of school and hardly at all on the last.

Both Julio and Cricket were going to be with Lucas in fourth grade. Lucas was glad that Cricket was going to be in his class. She didn't bug him the way she used to. In fact, he rather liked her. He would have been sorry if she was not in his class again.

Julio gave Lucas a high-five handshake when he discovered that they would be together. It would be the third year in a row they were in the same class.

Then Mrs. Hockaday opened her shopping bag and began to take out the prizes. Lucas could see that they were all the same size, and all of them were wrapped in the same red, white, and blue wrapping paper. Then Mrs. Hockaday began calling out names.

"Cricket Kaufman, who worked the hardest," she said. Lucas felt a stab of disappointment. If Mrs. Hockaday was calling out names in alphabetical order, he had already lost his chance of getting a prize.

Cricket ran up and grabbed her prize. It was three brand-new pencils. One of them was half red and half blue so you could sharpen it at both ends and write in two colors.

Pencils weren't such a great prize, thought Lucas. It wasn't such a big deal that he wasn't getting a prize.

"Arthur Lewis, for most improved work," said Mrs. Hockaday.

"Julio Sanchez, our best athlete." It was true. Besides his skill at cartwheels and handstands, Julio could run faster and throw a ball harder than anyone else in the class.

"Sara Jane Cushman, for the neatest work," said Mrs. Hockaday.

Suddenly, Lucas realized that Sara Jane's name had not been called in alphabetical order. There was still a chance that his name would be called after all.

One by one, Mrs. Hockaday called out the names of the students. Everyone got the same prize—three pencils and one of them was half red and half blue.

Every other student seemed to have gotten a prize. Lucas tried not to care. What did he need those old pencils for anyhow?

"Lucas Cott," called out Mrs. Hockaday. Everyone sat very still. What could Lucas be getting a prize for?

"Lucas Cott," repeated Mrs. Hockaday, "for the best improved conduct at the end of the year."

Mrs. Hockaday smiled at Lucas as she handed him his package, and Lucas smiled back at her. Then he tore off the red, white, and blue wrapping paper and admired his pencils. He was very pleased to have them, just like everyone else.

"Have a wonderful summer," Mrs. Hockaday told her students. "When you walk back into the school in September, you will all be fourth graders. I hope you will work hard and show your new teachers how much you learned in third grade."

"Of course we will," said Cricket Kaufman, and everyone agreed with her.

The bell rang for dismissal and Lucas rushed to leave the room with his classmates. But Mrs. Hockaday called his name one last time. "Please give this note to your parents," she said, handing him a folded piece of paper.

Lucas took the pink paper and waited until he got out on the street to open it. He wondered what Mrs. Hockaday was going to say about him now.

He read: "Lucas is no longer the rambunctious student he once was."

Teachers sure knew a lot of big words, Lucas thought as he tried to decode the message. *Ram-*

bunctious had never been on a vocabulary list either. He saw Cricket walking ahead and considered asking her for help. But even though she had been given a prize, Mrs. Hockaday didn't call her the smartest in the class. And Lucas remembered that she hadn't been right about the word in the note earlier in the year.

Rambunctious. A ram was a male sheep. Maybe the note said he was no longer like a sheep. Lucas put his hand to his head and laughed. Just yesterday he had gone to the barbershop again and gotten a short summer haircut. Of course he was no longer a sheep. Teachers sure were funny.

And he hurried home with the pink note, the yellow report card, and the three pencils—including the one that was half red and half blue.

ABOUT THE AUTHOR

JOHANNA HURWITZ is the author of many popular books for young readers, including *Aldo Applesauce*, *Rip-Roaring Russell*, and *The Adventures of Ali Baba Bernstein*. She has worked as a children's librarian in school and public libraries in New York City and on Long Island. And she frequently visits schools around the country to talk about books with students, teachers, librarians, and parents.

Ms. Hurwitz and her husband live in Great Neck, New York. They are the parents of two grown children.

Stories that tickle your funny bone!

More books by
JOHANNA HURWITZ

Apple® Paperbacks

❏ NR42922-1	The Adventures of Ali Baba Bernstein	$2.50
❏ NR42619-2	The Cold and Hot Winter	$2.75
❏ NR43128-5	Dede Takes Charge!	$2.75
❏ NR42858-6	The Hot and Cold Summer	$2.75
❏ NR43169-2	Hurray for Ali Baba Bernstein	$2.75
❏ NR40766-X	Hurricane Elaine	$2.50

Little Apple® Paperbacks

❏ NR41821-1	Class Clown	$2.50
❏ NR42031-3	Teacher's Pet	$2.50

LITTLE ★ APPLE®

BABY-SITTERS

Little Sister®

by Ann M. Martin, author of *The Baby-sitters Club®*

❑	MQ44300-3	#1	Karen's Witch	$2.75
❑	MQ44259-7	#2	Karen's Roller Skates	$2.75
❑	MQ44299-7	#3	Karen's Worst Day	$2.75
❑	MQ44264-3	#4	Karen's Kittycat Club	$2.75
❑	MQ44258-9	#5	Karen's School Picture	$2.75
❑	MQ43651-1	#10	Karen's Grandmothers	$2.75
❑	MQ43650-3	#11	Karen's Prize	$2.75
❑	MQ43649-X	#12	Karen's Ghost	$2.75
❑	MQ43648-1	#13	Karen's Surprise	$2.75
❑	MQ43646-5	#14	Karen's New Year	$2.75
❑	MQ43645-7	#15	Karen's In Love	$2.75
❑	MQ43644-9	#16	Karen's Goldfish	$2.75
❑	MQ43643-0	#17	Karen's Brothers	$2.75
❑	MQ43642-2	#18	Karen's Home-Run	$2.75
❑	MQ43641-4	#19	Karen's Good-Bye	$2.95
❑	MQ44823-4	#20	Karen's Carnival	$2.75
❑	MQ44824-2	#21	Karen's New Teacher	$2.95
❑	MQ44833-1	#22	Karen's Little Witch	$2.95
❑	MQ44832-3	#23	Karen's Doll	$2.95
❑	MQ44859-5	#24	Karen's School Trip	$2.75
❑	MQ44831-5	#25	Karen's Pen Pal	$2.75
❑	MQ44830-7	#26	Karen's Ducklings	$2.75
❑	MQ44829-3	#27	Karen's Big Joke	$2.75
❑	MQ44828-5	#28	Karen's Tea Party	$2.75
❑	MQ44825-0	#29	Karen's Cartwheel	$2.75
❑	MQ45645-8	#30	Karen's Kittens	$2.75
❑	MQ45646-6	#31	Karen's Bully	$2.95
❑	MQ45647-4	#32	Karen's Pumpkin Patch	$2.95
❑	MQ45648-2	#33	Karen's Secret	$2.95
❑	MQ45650-4	#34	Karen's Snow Day	$2.95
❑	MQ45652-0	#35	Karen's Doll Hosital	$2.95